Welcome To Squad
Activity Book For Swimmers
By AlyT

Written by AlyT
© Copyright 2024 by Allison Tyson. All rights reserved.

First printing: April, 2024

Disclaimer
While we draw on our professional expertise and background in teaching learn to swim and swimming training, by purchasing and reading our products you acknowledge that we have produced this book for informational and educational purposes only. You alone are solely responsible and take full responsibility for your own wellbeing as well as the health, lives and well-being of your family and children in your care in and around water.

Stay in touch:
Born to Swim, P.O Box 6699, Cairns City, QLD 4870
SwimMechanics@yahoo.com
www.BornToSwim.com.au
www.PoweredByChlorine.com
Instagram @LearnToSwimTheAustralianWay
Etsy Store www.borntoswimglobal.etsy.com
Most titles available from Etsy, Amazon and all good online Book Retailers

Other titles by this Author:
Water Awareness Newborns
Water Awareness Babies
Water Awareness Toddlers
Learn to Swim the Australian Way Level 1 The Foundations
Learn to Swim the Australian Way Level 2 The Basics
Learn to Swim the Australian Way Level 3 Intermediate
Learn to Swim the Australian Way Level 4 Advanced
The Ultimate Pool Party Planner
Focus On Freestyle: Teaching Guide
Water Safety: Teaching Guide
Breaststroke Bootcamp: Teaching Guide
Butterfly Bootcamp: Teaching Guide
Backstroke Bootcamp: Teaching Guide
Learning To Float: Color Me In & Learn To Swim Activity Book
A Float For Every Stroke: Teaching Body Position
Visual Aids For Inclusive Aquatic Education: 100+ Swimming Flashcards
Welcome To Swim Squad: Activity Book For Swimmers
Welcome To Water Safety: Activity Book For Swimmers
Eat Pray Swim: A Swimmer's Logbook & Prayer Journal
Thalassophile: Logbook & Journal For Lovers Of The Ocean and Sea
Competitive Swimming Quotes: Coloring Book For Adults & Teens
Wild Swimming Quotes: Coloring Book For Adults & Teens
Mermaids: Coloring Book For Adults & Teens
Powered By Chlorine : Logbooks & Journals For Swimmers

NAME:
☐

WELCOME TO SWIM SQUAD

© borntoswim.com.au

For the swim kids & coaches!

This totally awesome, very handy and long overdue activity book is the ultimate guide to preparing swimmers to join a swimming squad.

We created this nifty workbook for coaches, swim parents and swimmers to give them a little insight into the nuts and bolts of swimming in a squad.
Plus it's great for getting everyone's heads together and working as a team! Shweet!!

No dull diagrams! We packed quite a bit inside (crossword puzzles, word search and missing word challenges, word jumbles...blah blah) all designed to make the transition into squad training a breeze.
Seriously, there's something in here for everyone, you'll be learning heaps smashing it in no time, and spoiler alert! the answers are in the back for those really tricky challenges that even a few coaches and swim mom and dads will get stuck on too!!

But that's not all! The big feature of this workbook is we added a pile of things every swimmer NEEDS to know before they get to the pool - stuff like lane etiquette, using a pace clock, swimming myths, training zones!?, the different phases of freestyle, common coaching jargon and WAY MORE!

Plus, you'll learn about the must-have gear and training tools used at squad training and we threw in a handy checklist so you won't forget anything for your first swim meet. Boom...you're welcome :)

Get ready to take your swimming skills to the next level!
Jump in and let's make a splash together!
Sharing swimming awesomeness

Alyt

By the way...if you love this book blow up the comments & give us some

★★★★★

Stay in the loop! Follow us on your favourite socials!
 Insta @learntoswimtheaustralianway   E Etsy www.borntoswimglobal.etsy.com    Facebook @swimmechanics

Be sure to drop us a like if you find our stuff helpful

www.poweredbychlorine.com
And if you're looking for some cool gear to spiffy up your training experience, be sure to check out our store

A QUICK RUNDOWN OF WHAT'S INSIDE

Introducing ... 1

A little About Me ... 4

Welcome To Squad - Color In ... 5

Training Gear Essentials - Image Match Ups ... 7

Common Swimming Phrases - Missing Words ... 8

Swimming Slang Showdown - Word Match Up ... 9

Find My Gear - Maze ... 10

The 5th Stroke - Missing Word ... 11

Swim Squad Essentials - Word Search ... 12

Backstroke - Quiz ... 13

Different Stokes - Crossword ... 14

The Pace Clock - Color In ... 15

What's Our Swimmer Doing? - Image Match Up ... 17

Phases of Freestyle - Missing Words ... 18

Lane Line Labyrinth - Maze ... 19

Odd Ways To Train - Image Match Up ... 20

Streamline Divers - Color In ... 21

Lane Etiquette - Missing Words ... 23

Swimming Myth Buster - Quiz ... 24

Find Their Fins - Maze ... 25

Pace Clock Facts - Missing Words ... 26

Design Your Own Swimmer & Swim Wear - Color In ... 27

Breaststroke Brain Buster - Word Association ... 29

What's My Time - Quiz ... 30

Race Finish & Turns Challenge - Multiple Choice ... 31

Get In The Zone - Word Association ... 32

Locate Your Locker - Maze ... 33

Butterfly True & False - Quiz ... 34

Training Aids - Word Search ... 35

The I.M - Crossword ... 36

Jumbled Jargon - Word Scramble ... 37

Carnival Kit - Guided Checklist ... 38

Answers ... 39 - 43

WELCOME TO SQUAD

SWIMMING TRAINING

We left this page empty on purpose so your colors don't mess up the next page after you've finished coloring. You can use this blank page to let your creativity flow and create your own swimming masterpiece!!

1. Training Gear Essentials

Can you match and name the training gear?

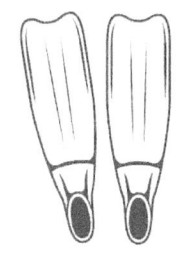   •   • mesh bag

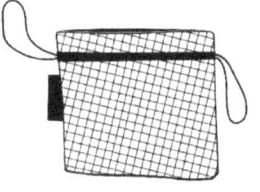   •   • pull buoy

   •   • swimming cap

   •   • long fins

   •   • kickboard

   •   • hand paddles

   •   • goggles

2. COMMON SWIMMING PHRASES
YOU'RE LIKELY TO HEAR AT TRAINING

Fill in the coaching phrase with the missing words

1- Leave with your .... on the wall.

2- The clock doesn't .... unless you .... the wall.

3- Pass on the ....

4- Tighten your ....

5- Keep your .... high.

6- .... for the water.

8- Drive from your ....

9- Pace ....

10- Start on the ....

yourself   streamline   touch   feet
stop   top   feel   elbows   hips   outside

3. Swimming Slang Showdown

Different squads often use different words to describe the same swimming equipment and jargon. Match up the swimming jargon so you never get confused.

pull-buoy	lane line
flip flops	stitch
flippers	frog stroke
gym workout	rashie
swimwear	thongs
bands	boardies
trunks	swimming instructor
swim gear	tent
sun-shirt	club
breaststroke	pool equipment
swim teacher	dryland training
lane rope	buoy
sweats	togs
swim meet	swim kit
team	ankle straps
swimming gear	change rooms
parka	swimming carnival
kit	hoodie
locker room	fins
marque	gear
cramp	track pants

4. FIND MY GEAR

Draw a line and help the swim mom, swimmer, lifeguard and coach find their gear.

5. THE 5TH STROKE

GUESS THE MISSING WORD

━ ━ ━ ━ ━ ━ ━ ━ ━ ━ ━ ━ ━

1. When you dive into the pool, before breaking out to the surface, what do you do to move quickly underwater?
2. What type of kicking do you do when you push off the wall before you begin to swim?
3. After completing a turn, what technique helps you move efficiently underwater?
4. During backstroke starts, what do you do after pushing off the wall to move quickly underwater before coming to the surface?
5. What is the fifth stroke in swimming, involving powerful kicking underwater?
6. What term describes the technique where a swimmer is completely submerged at the end of a backstroke race?

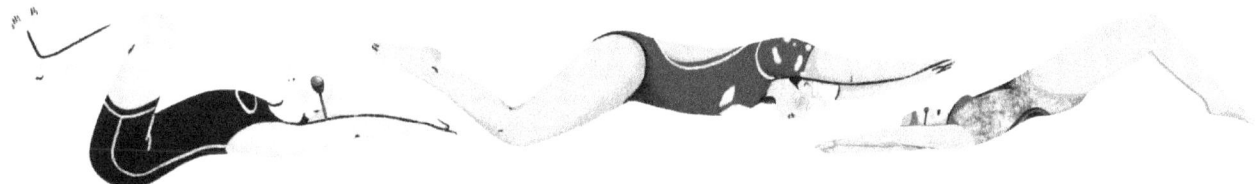

6. SWIM SQUAD ESSENTIALS
WORD SEARCH

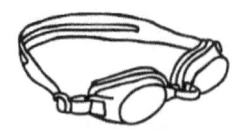

Fill your kit bag by finding the words from the list below.

s	h	c	l	y	m	a	w	s	w
w	r	x	s	o	b	f	g	h	a
i	s	o	s	u	l	e	w	o	t
m	e	s	h	b	a	g	k	r	e
s	w	p	y	l	s	o	y	t	r
u	h	t	i	l	u	g	e	f	b
i	s	a	o	u	s	g	o	i	o
t	c	c	a	p	e	l	m	n	t
j	d	u	z	s	j	e	s	s	t
b	v	t	n	q	p	s	m	i	l
k	i	c	k	b	o	a	r	d	e

mesh bag   kickboard   water bottle
towel   goggles   short fins
cap   pull buoy   swimsuit

7. BACKSTROKE TRUE OR FALSE

WHEN SWIMMING BACKSTROKE, SWIMMERS SHOULD KEEP THEIR KNEES AND FEET UNDER THE WATER?

SWIMMERS ARE ALLOWED TO DIVE FROM THE BLOCKS IN BACKSTROKE RACES?

THE FLAGS ACROSS THE POOL ARE FOR SWIMMERS TO GRAB OR DIVE OVER?

SWIMMERS MUST SWIM ON THEIR BACKS DURING THE ENTIRE BACKSTROKE RACE, EXCEPT DURING TURNS?

SWIMMERS ARE ALLOWED TO STAY UNDERWATER FOR AS LONG AS THEY CAN HOLD THEIR BREATH AFTER EACH BACKSTROKE START AND TURN?

BACKSTROKE IS THE ONLY STROKE WHERE SWIMMERS START IN THE WATER, NOT ON THE STARTING BLOCKS?

SWIMMERS ARE ALLOWED TO PULL ON THE LANE LINES DURING BACKSTROKE RACES TO HELP GUIDE THEIR SWIMMING?

SWIMMERS MUST TOUCH THE WALL WITH BOTH HANDS WHEN BACKSTROKE RACES END?

IF YOU BEND YOUR ARMS DURING BACKSTROKE YOU WILL GET DISQUALIFIED?

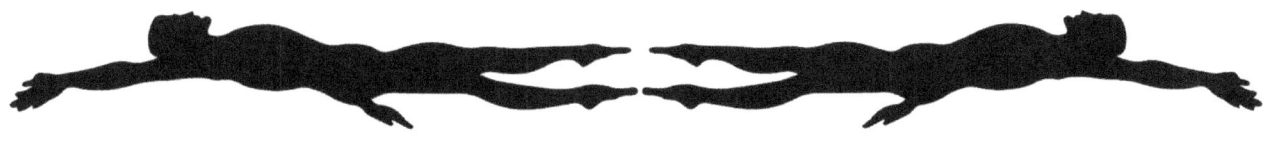

8. DIFFERENT STROKES

CROSSWORD PUZZLE

ACROSS

1. performed after diving in, pushing off or turning at the wall
2. another name for butterfly
3. an important element of every facet of swimming
4. race name made up of four team members

DOWN

5. underwater phase of the breaststroke start
6. aquatic mammal name for the butterfly kick
7. another name for freestyle
8. sometimes referred to as frog stroke
9. the transition from being under water to starting the initial strokes

© borntoswim.com.au

THE PACE CLOCK

A pace clock is a large analog clock found at swimming pools, unlike regular clocks they have only one long hand divided into two colors. Swimmers and coaches use the pace clock to regulate swimmer's intervals, rest periods, and gauge performance.

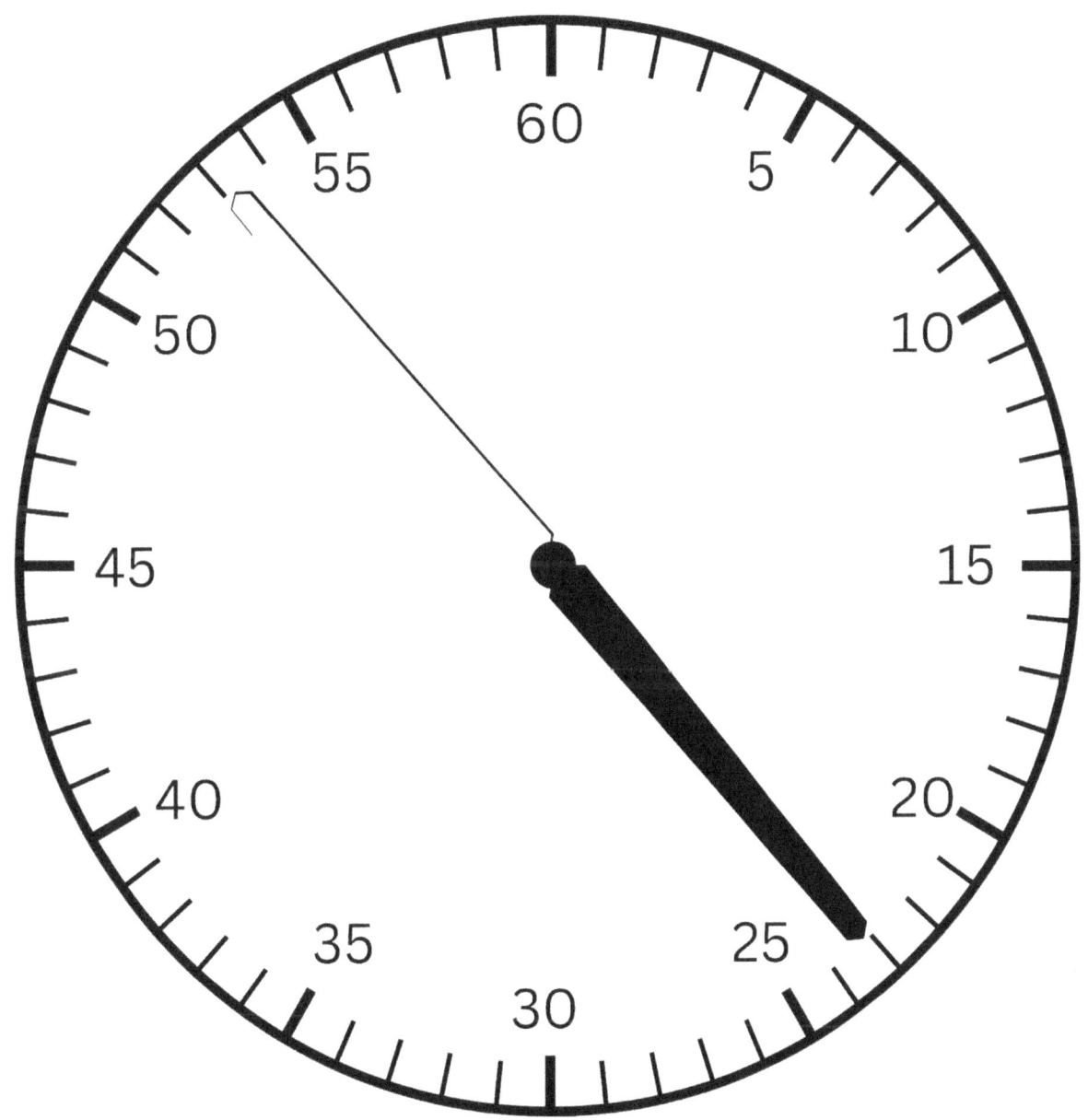

Find the pace clock at your pool. Color in the pace clock in your book to match the colors of the real pace clock you found at the pool.

We left this page empty on purpose so your colors don't mess up the next page after you've finished coloring. You can use this blank page to let your creativity flow and create your own swimming masterpiece!!

9. What's our swimmer doing?

Draw a line to match and name each of the swimming skills.

   Kick Sets

   Backstroke

   Relay

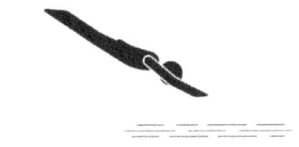   Open Water Start

   Butterfly

   Racing Start

   Breaststroke

   Dive

   Freestyle

10. Phases of Freestyle
MISSING WORDS

Choose the correct word to fill-in-the blanks in the sentences which describe each part of freestyle

KICK	RECOVERY	ROTATION	CATCH
ENTRY	PULL	SIX
CATCH	FINISH	EXTENSION	PROPULSION

1. The ____ is the phase of the freestyle arm action where the hand enters the water in front of the head.

2. It is important to relax the hand during the _____ as the arm moves over the water.

3. The release, also known as the _____ is the phase of freestyle where the hand exits the water.

4. Continuous leg _____ during freestyle is often referred to as a ___ beat ____ .

5. Once the hand re-enters the water the hand should be placed in the _____ position before starting the ____ .

6. Adding _____ to freestyle enhances technique, power, and efficiency.

7. The _____ phase, maximizes the swimmer's reach to help set up for an effective _____ .

Identify each of the different phases of FREESTYLE

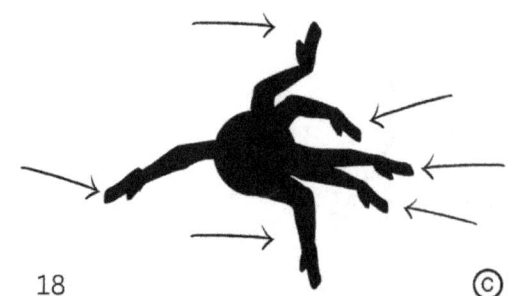

11. Lane Line Labyrinth

Find your way to the wall.
Don't forget to 'touch the wall' when you get there!

12. Odd Ways To Train!

Some swimmers use advanced equipment when they swim, this challenges them and isolates skills so they can build strength and swim faster.

Match and name the advanced equipment the swimmers are using.

   Wearing drag socks

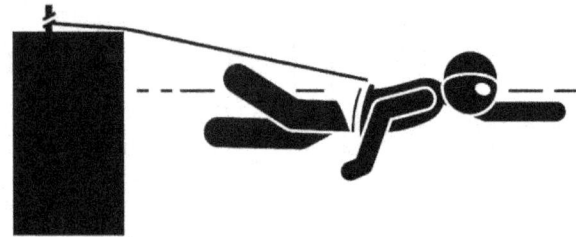   Sculling with a snorkel

   Swimming with hand paddles

   Using a resistance belt or bungee

   Swimming with a resistance parachute

© borntoswim.com.au

STREAMLINE DIVERS

To get super good at diving, swimmers need to learn to streamline as they enter the water. Swimmers also use the same streamline pose every time they push off from the wall. Practice your "streamline pose" by:

1. stack your hands one on top of the other and lock them with your thumbs
2. stretch your arms up and above your head
3. keep your arms pressed against or behind your ears
4. keep your feet together and point your toes
5. stretch and make yourself as long and as flat as you can

We left this page empty on purpose so your colors don't mess up the next page after you've finished coloring. You can use this blank page to let your creativity flow and create your own swimming masterpiece!!

13. LANE ETIQUETTE

MATCH THE MISSING PHRASES TO THE SENTENCES, FOR A BETTER TRAINING EXPERIENCE FOR EVERYONE!!

move to the side	avoid colliding	T	other swimmers	lane ropes	finishes
bump	approaching	dive in	finish and touch	continuing	false start
line	mid-lane	end	outside	plastic floats	hand
to the side	resurfacing point	circle	direction	target point	oncoming
turn	backstroke flags	legs	prevent collisions	speed up	wall

During training, always swim to the side of the contrasting .... down the middle of the lane. It helps you swim straight and avoid collisions.

The underwater .... at the end of the lane helps you know you are approaching the wall and when to ....

The .... rope across the pool is there to help stop a race if someone goes too early.

When swimming backstroke count your strokes from the .... to know where the wall is, this way, you won't .... your head.

The .... are cables covered with small .... they have a contrasting color to indicate the .... and to help swimmers see they are .... the end of the lane.

When you .... the lane, you swim in a clock-wise or counter-clockwise .... This way, you won't bump into .... swimmers.

When training, never stop .... to fix goggles, roll onto your back, or wait until you reach the .... of the lane.

To pass other swimmers, never grab their .... Always pass on the .... People being passed should not .... , and should always move closer to the lane rope. This helps ....

Always start your set with your feet touching the .... , and always touch the wall with your .... or hands when you finish a set. This gives you a chance to practice your race ....

When sharing a lane in training, as you finish a set, stop and .... so the next swimmer can .... the wall.

When .... to swim, turn at the .... - centered on the wall at the end of each lane then move immediately .... of the lane to .... with other swimmers.

Never .... unless the coach tells you to. Remember to ALWAYS look for swimmers before diving in, so you don't hurt ....

14. SWIMMING MYTH BUSTER

Circle TRUE / FALSE to see if you can unravel some common swimming myths!

- T / F You should be able to see your knees break the surface when you kick on your back?

- T / F Swimmers don't sweat?

- T / F Swimming can turn your hair green?

- T / F Swimming straight after eating a big lunch or milkshake will give you cramps?

- T / F You should always sprint the warm-up?

- T / F You should wait 15-30 minutes after applying sunscreen before going for a swim?

- T / F The best swimmers hold their breath?

- T / F It's OK to pee in the pool because everyone does it?

- T / F Drills are a great way to pass the time and think about what's for dinner?

- T / F Using a pull-buoy is a way for coach to let you rest your legs?

- T / F Going too deep underwater can cause an ear infection?

- T / F Swimming in a long-sleeve rashie can slow you down and make it hard to swim?

- T / F There is only one way to swim freestyle?

- T / F Swimming makes you sleepy and hungry?

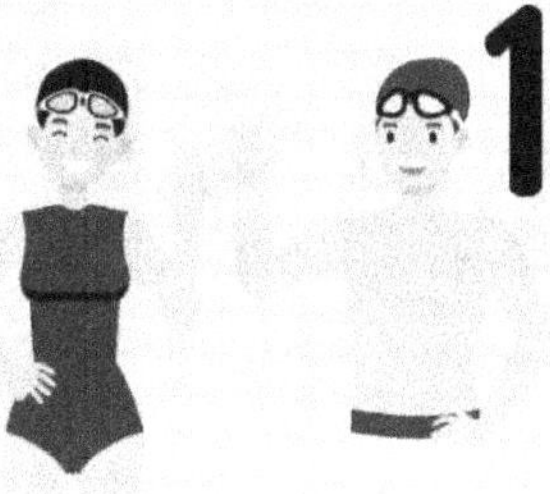

15. MAZE GAME

Help the swimmers find their fins

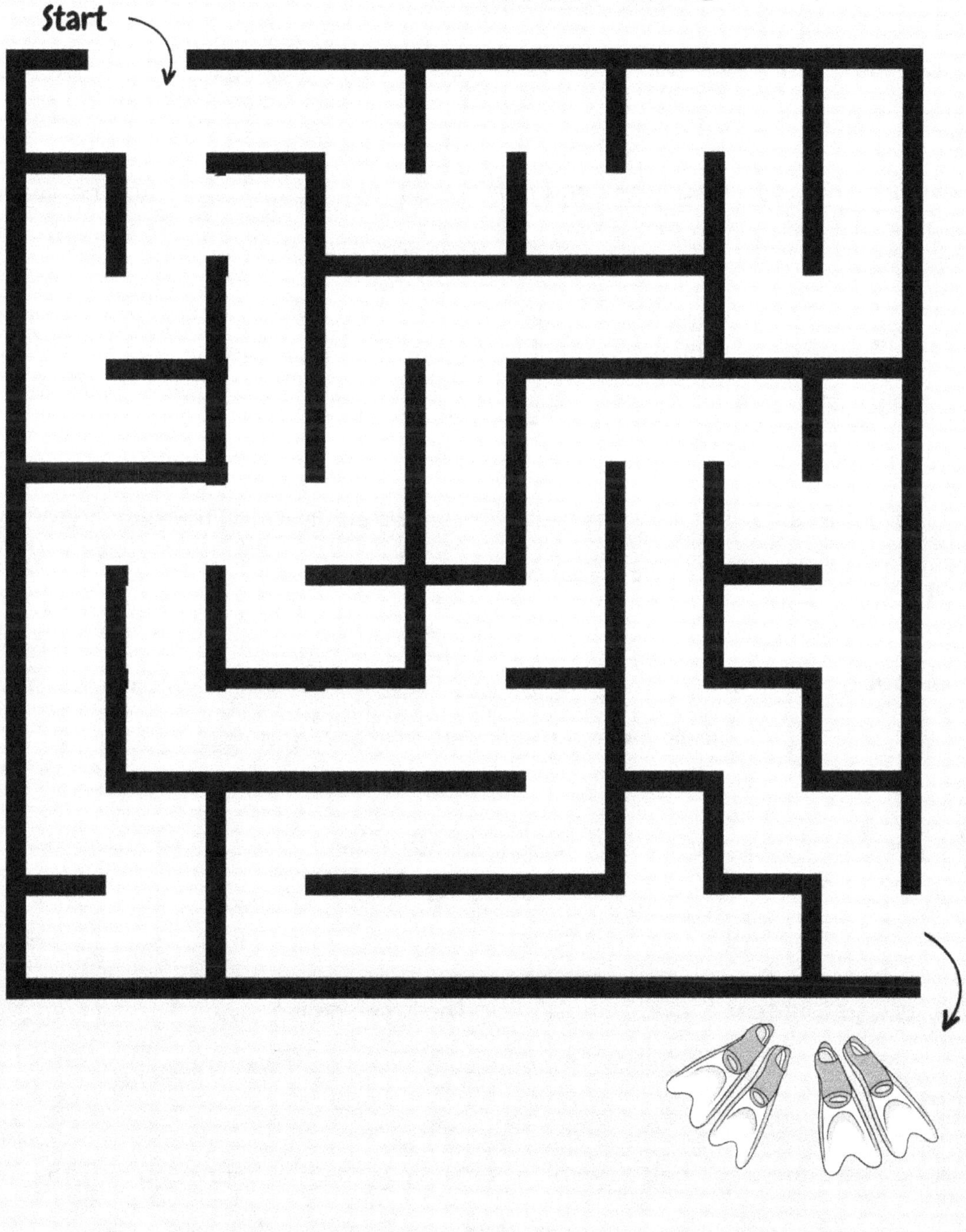

16. PACE CLOCK FACTS & PHRASES

track top hand leave progress 30 intervals
seconds speed space feedback

FIND THE MISSING WORDS TO LEARN MORE ABOUT THE PACE CLOCK.

Leave On The Top: When the hand points to the "..................." or 60 the swimmers begins their swim.

Leave On The Bottom: When the hand points to the "Bottom" or ...., swimmers begin their swim.

The time between swims or swimmers, often determined by the coach and the pace clock, is known as '...................'.

Second spacing is when the '...................' moves forward before the next swimmer starts their swim, ensuring consistent intervals.

The pace clock helps swimmers '...................' out their '...................' times, maintaining control and consistency in rest intervals.

Swimmers get instant '...................' on their swimming '...................' from the pace clock, helping them assess their performance

Using the pace clock helps swimmers see how they're improving and they can '...................' their '...................'.

DESIGN YOUR OWN SWIMMER & SWIM WEAR

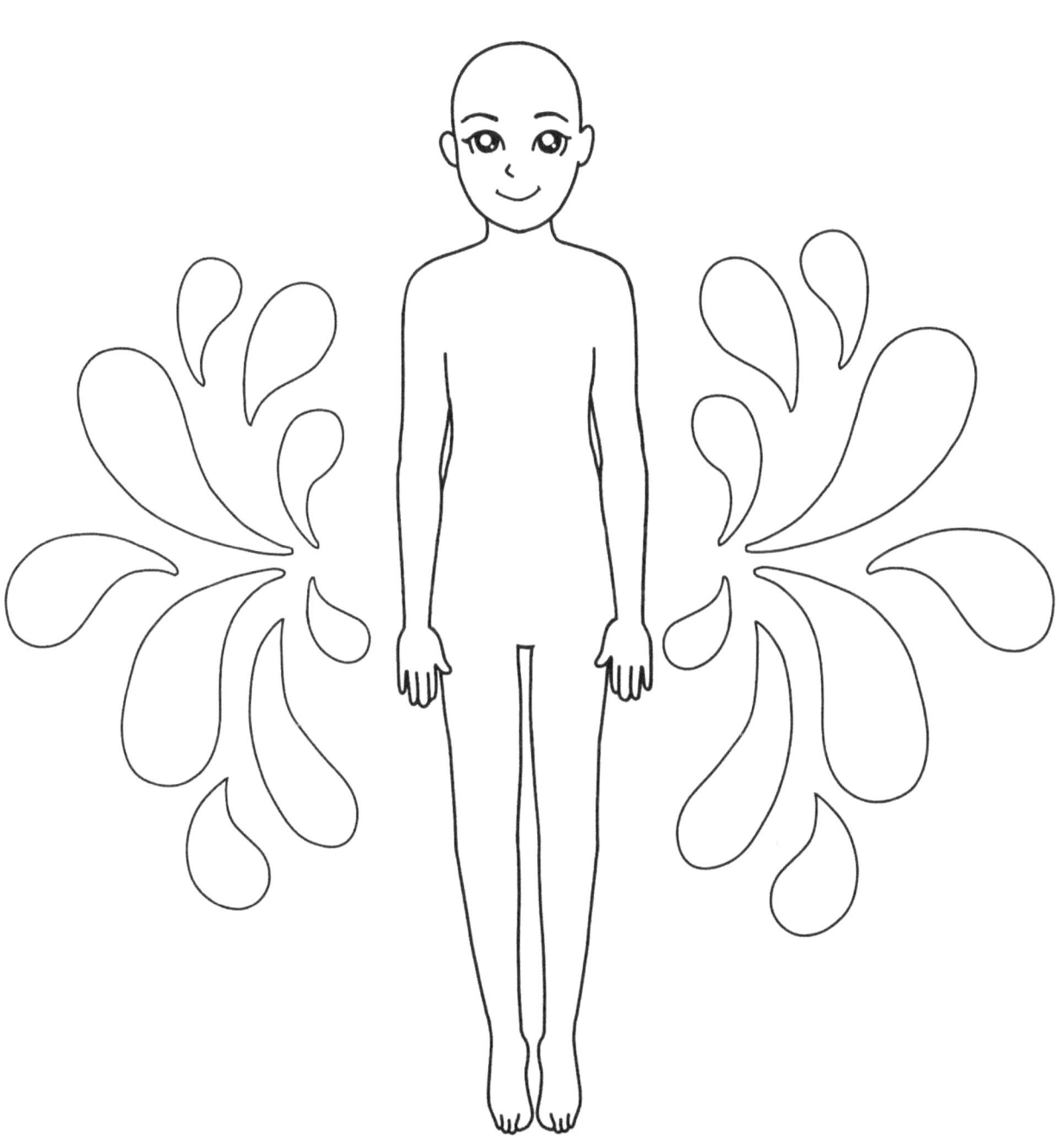

We left this page empty on purpose so your colors don't mess up the next page after you've finished coloring. You can use this blank page to let your creativity flow and create your own swimming masterpiece!!

17. BREASTSTROKE Brain Buster
test your knowledge on breaststroke technique

shoot recovery insweep frog outsweep glide

1 Question: What is the name given to describe the breaststroke kick to younger swimmers? Answer:

2 Question: What is the phase of the breaststroke where the arms extend forward in front of the swimmer and pause for a moment? Answer:

3 Question: What phase follows the momentary pause and the hands start to move outward? Answer:

4 Question: What is the term for the phase where the hands change direction and push water toward the chest to propel the swimmer forward? Answer:

5 Question: Following the propulsive phase, what motion brings the arms back to the starting position? Answer:

6 Question: What is the action of driving the hands forward often referred to as? Answer:

18. WHAT'S MY TIME?

At first, using the pace clock might seem tricky, but it's actually super helpful for swimmers because it can help make you swim faster and feel more confident in the pool

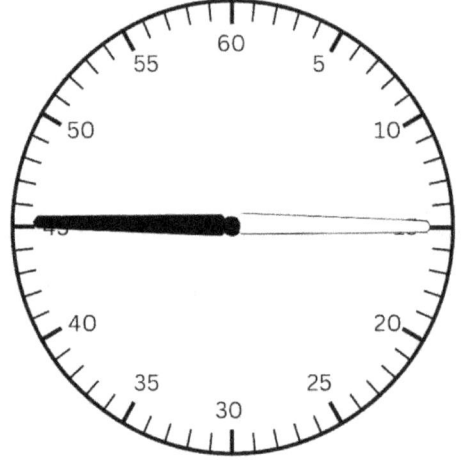

If swimmers leave in intervals of 5s, and the lead swimmer leaves on the 30, on what number will the second swimmer leave the wall on?

A:

If a swimmer takes 30 seconds to complete their swim and they touch the wall when the white hand reads '15'. What number was the white hand pointing to when they pushed off from the wall?

B:

If a swimmer leaves on the 15 and touches the wall on the 50, what was their time for their swim?

D:

If the lead swimmer leaves on the 60 and the next swimmer leaves 10s after, what number did the second swimmer leave on?

C:

If a swimmer leaves on the top and takes 45s to swim their lap, how much rest do they get before they leave on the top again?

E:

19. Race Finish and Turn Challenge

A great race finish or turn at the wall can make all the difference in a swim meet.
Do you know each of the different turns and finishes as you're coming into the wall?
Check your knowledge by answering each of the multiple choice questions.

How many hands do you touch the wall with for a freestyle finish?
a) One hand
b) Two hands
c) Two hands & a foot
d) No hands

Which strokes have a finish, where both hands must touch the wall simultaneously?
a) Backstroke & Freestyle
b) Breaststroke & Backstroke
c) Butterfly & Breaststroke
d) Freestyle & Butterfly

What is the technique used for the butterfly-to-backstroke turn?
a) Flip turn
b) Open turn
c) Back flip
d) Tumble turn

In breaststroke, what is the rule for the finish?
a) Hands must be separated and touch the wall simultaneously
b) Both hands need to be at the exact same height when they touch the wall
c) Hands must overlap one on top of the other when they touch the wall
d) The swimmer can touch the wall with any part of their body

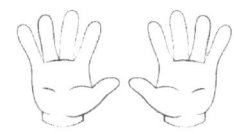

Which turn involves a transition from swimming on your back to swimming on your front?
a) Backstroke to breaststroke turn
b) Breaststroke to freestyle turn
c) Butterfly turn
d) Breaststroke turn

Which two strokes commonly use flip turns to change direction at the wall?
a) Butterfly & Backstroke
b) Backstroke & Breaststroke
c) Breaststroke & Freestyle
d) Backstroke & Freestyle

A tumble turn is a different name for which of the two turns?
a) Flip turn and front flip
b) Open turn and back flip
c) Back flip and flip turn
d) Open turn and cross over turn

20. GET IN THE ZONE

Training intensity zones are like different levels of effort when you exercise. They help you know how hard you should be working during workouts to get the best results. There are different zones that help you pace and push yourself just enough to improve your fitness and reach your goals.
By understanding and using these zones, you can make your workouts more effective and enjoyable.

.... Zone 1 (Easy Swim): This zone is for easy swimming, like when you're cooling down after a hard practice or catching your breath between faster swims. You swim at a relaxed pace, feeling comfortable.

.... Zone 2 (Steady Swim): This is when you swim a comfortable, steady pace and feel like you can swim for a long time without getting too tired or needing a break. It's a great zone to swim a long, distance set in practice.

.... Zone 3 (Challenge Yourself): In this zone, you swim a bit faster than usual, but not as fast as you can go. You should feel challenged but not completely out of breath.

.... Zone 4 (Push Your Limits): This zone is tough! You're swimming as fast as you can, pushing yourself to go faster. It's great for building speed and strength and you should feel like you're breathing really hard and can't keep up this pace for long.

.... Zone 5 (Give It Everything): This is your all-out effort zone! You're swimming as fast as you possibly can, giving it everything you've got. You can only keep this pace for a very short time, like when you're sprinting to the finish line in a race.

Vo2 Max   Threshold   Aerobic
Maximum Effort   Recovery

21. LOCATE YOUR LOCKER MAZE

Most swimming pools have a locker room where swimmers can get changed in and out of their swim gear and use the bathroom facilities. Different countries refer to their locker rooms with names like change rooms, bathrooms, dressing sheds etc.
What do they call them at your pool? ....

22. BUTTERFLY TRUE OR FALSE

Butterfly kick is often referred to as dolphin kick?

There are only two kicks during the butterfly stroke cycle?

You should keep your eyes looking forward at all times when swimming butterfly?

It's ok if you swap the butterfly kick for the breaststroke kick when swimming butterfly if you get tired?

Swimming butterfly can help you swim better freestyle?

You should dive down as deep as you can when swimming butterfly?

The wave-like motion performed during butterfly is called the undulation?

The butterfly landing position is often referred to as the chest press?

Another name for swimming butterfly is the lady bird?

When swimming butterfly it is best to time the kicks with the hands as they enter and exit the water?

During the butterfly stroke, swimmers use a flutter kick?

When swimming butterfly, it's important to keep your head low and your body close to the water's surface?

Both hands exit the water near the hips when swimming butterfly?

Swimmers should pause and glide after the hands enter the water and before kicking during the butterfly stroke cycle?

23. TRAINING AIDS WORD SEARCH

Can you find the 10 training aids hidden in the puzzle?

paddles   nose clip   ear plugs   snorkel   tempo trainer   logbook
jammers   stopwatch   ankle strap   flippers

```
T  B  J  W  N  B  T  L  C  A  P  S
C  E  A  P  F  I  R  O  S  T  A  C
P  C  M  A  S  M  A  G  N  P  D  A
A  K  M  P  T  W  U  B  C  I  D  F
R  P  E  S  O  L  D  O  A  L  L  L
T  A  R  T  P  T  N  O  N  C  E  I
S  C  S  R  W  R  R  K  A  E  S  P
E  K  A  C  A  M  P  A  R  S  P  P
L  E  U  M  T  K  I  N  I  O  Q  E
K  L  A  S  C  L  I  G  H  N  A  R
N  R  E  C  H  F  O  V  L  S  E  S
A  S  N  O  R  K  E  L  G  B  A  R
```

24. The I.M CROSSWORD PUZZLE

Test Your I.M Knowledge

1. First word of the I.M
2. Third stroke of the I.M
3. How many of the competitive strokes are performed on the back?
4. First stroke of the I.M
5. Second word of the I.M
6. How much of the race does the swimmer swim in each style in the I.M?
7. Second stroke of the I.M
8. Term for when a swimmer switches from one stroke to another in the I.M
9. Number of different strokes swum in the I.M
10. Last stroke of the I.M
11. Common place swimmers can lose speed
12. Event consisting of four team members swimming different strokes in the same race

25. Jumbled Jargon

These jumbled words and meanings for advanced training terms should provide a fun challenge, but warning you may need some (or a lot) of help from your coach, parents or an older sibling to unjumble and explain them!!

2vo mxa : The maximum amount of oxygen a person can use during intense exercise. It's like the engine capacity of a car!

tievaeng ltspi : Swimming the second half of a race faster than the first half. It's like pacing yourself to finish strong!

tnesdaci epr rtkose : How far you travel with each stroke. It's like measuring how efficient your swimming is!

snaptoler ebsp : Your fastest time ever in a race. It's like beating your own record!

ahet tshee : A list of swimmers and their events at a swim meet. It's like your race schedule!

aeltinrsv : Training sessions divided into timed segments of work and rest. It's like taking breaks between swimming hard!

lctaate thredohls : The point during exercise where lactic acid builds up in your muscles. It's like when your muscles start to feel tired!

critcail wmis eespd : The pace at which you can swim continuously without getting tired too quickly. It's like finding your optimal swimming speed!

rahtaerte : The number of times your heart beats per minute. It's like a measure of how hard you're working!

trseko tare : The number of strokes you take per minute while swimming. It's like counting how fast you're arms are moving through the water

CARNIVAL KIT
CHECKLIST IDEAS FOR YOUR SWIM MEET

- [ ] LOCATION
- [ ] ARRIVAL TIME & TEAM BRIEFING
- [ ] WARM UP TIME
- [ ] HEAT SHEETS
- [ ] EVENT SCHEDULE
- [ ] FINISH TIME & TEAM DEBRIEF

CLOTHING & SHOES
- [ ] team apparel
- [ ] footwear
- [ ] parka or hoodie
- [ ] sweat pants
- [ ] sweatshirt
- [ ] warm socks
- [ ] hat
- [ ] change of clothes
- [ ] underwear
- [ ] ----------------------------
- [ ] ----------------------------
- [ ] ----------------------------

TOILETRIES
- [ ] shampoo
- [ ] conditioner
- [ ] shower gel
- [ ] moisturiser
- [ ] hair brush / comb
- [ ] hair ties + spare
- [ ] ----------------------------
- [ ] ----------------------------
- [ ] ----------------------------

RACE SWIM GEAR
- [ ] goggles + spare
- [ ] swimming cap + spare
- [ ] towel + spare
- [ ] swim bag
- [ ] swim wear
- [ ] ----------------------------
- [ ] ----------------------------
- [ ] ----------------------------
- [ ] ----------------------------

OTHER
- [ ] chairs x
- [ ] umbrella
- [ ] sunscreen
- [ ] rubbish bags
- [ ] first aid kit
- [ ] marker pen
- [ ] pencils x2
- [ ] blanket
- [ ] marque
- [ ] ID and wallet
- [ ] ----------------------------
- [ ] ----------------------------
- [ ] ----------------------------

FLUIDS & FUEL
- [ ] water bottle x
- [ ] snacks
- [ ] fruit
- [ ] ice
- [ ] pre-packed lunches
- [ ] ----------------------------
- [ ]

© borntoswim.com.au

Before searching the answers have a chat to your coach, parents, team mates or older siblings to find out more about each subject

1. Training Gear Essentials pg7

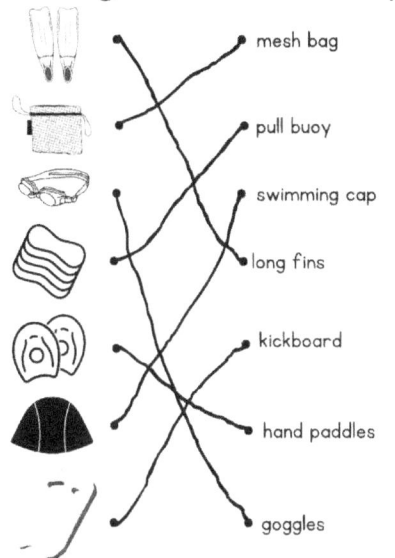

- mesh bag
- pull buoy
- swimming cap
- long fins
- kickboard
- hand paddles
- goggles

2. Common Swimming phrases pg8

1- Leave with your feet on the wall.
2- The clock doesn't stop unless you touch the wall.
3- Pass on the outside.
4- Tighten your streamline.
5- Keep your elbows high.
6- Feel for the water.
8- Drive from your hips.
9- Pace yourself.
10- Start on the top.

3. Swimming Slang Showdown pg9

- pull-buoy
- flip flops
- flippers
- gym workout
- swimwear
- bands
- trunks
- swim gear
- sun-shirt
- breaststroke
- swim teacher
- lane rope
- sweats
- swim meet
- team
- swimming gear
- parka
- kit
- locker room
- marque
- cramp

- lane line
- stitch
- frog stroke
- rashie
- thongs
- boardies
- swimming instructor
- tent
- club
- pool equipment
- dryland training
- buoy
- togs
- swim kit
- ankle straps
- change rooms
- swimming carnival
- hoodie
- fins
- gear
- track pants

4. Find my gear pg10

whistle   1st Aid   goggles   heat sheets

5. The 5th Stroke pg11
UNDERWATERS

6. Swim Squad Essentials pg12

s				y				s	w
w				o				h	a
i				u	l	e	w	o	t
m	e	s	h	b	a	g		r	e
s				l		o		t	r
u				l		g		f	b
i				u		g		i	o
t		c	a	p		l		n	t
						e		s	t
						s			l
k	i	c	k	b	o	a	r	d	e

7. Backstroke True or False pg13

When swimming backstroke, swimmers should keep their knees and feet under the water? **TRUE**

Swimmers are allowed to dive from the blocks in backstroke races? **FALSE**

The flags across the pool are for swimmers to grab or dive over? **FALSE**

Swimmers must swim on their backs during the entire backstroke race, except during turns? **TRUE**

Swimmers are allowed to stay underwater for as long as they can hold their breath after each backstroke start and turn? **FALSE**

Backstroke is the only stroke where swimmers start in the water, not on the starting blocks? **TRUE**

Swimmers are allowed to pull on the lane lines during backstroke races to help guide their swimming? **FALSE**

Swimmers must touch the wall with both hands when backstroke races end? **FALSE**

If you bend your arms during backstroke you will get disqualified? **FALSE**

8. Different Strokes pg14

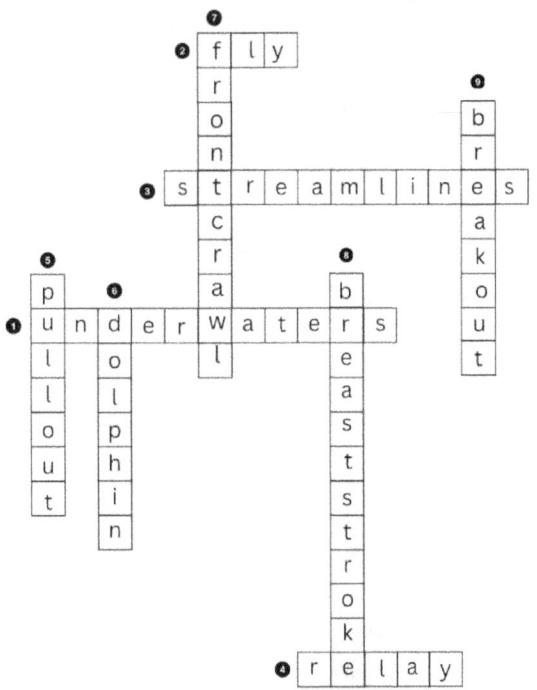

9. What's our swimmer doing? pg17

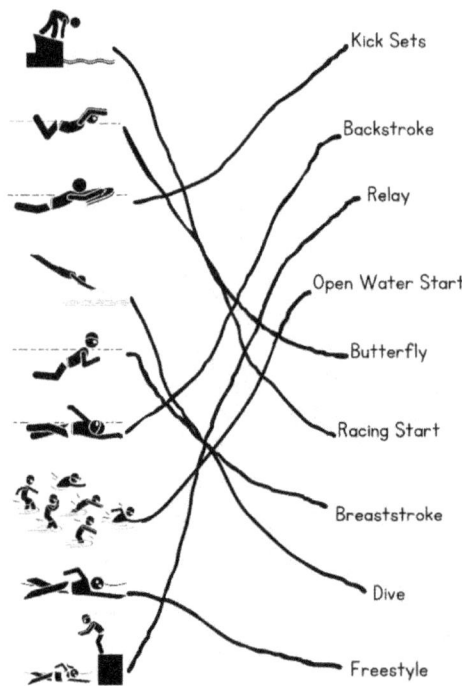

- Kick Sets
- Backstroke
- Relay
- Open Water Start
- Butterfly
- Racing Start
- Breaststroke
- Dive
- Freestyle

10. Phases of freestyle pg18

1. The ENTRY is the phase of the freestyle arm action where the hand enters the water in front of the head.
2. It is important to relax the hand during the RECOVERY as the arm moves over the water.
3. The release, also known as FINISH is the phase of freestyle where the hand exits the water.
4. Continuous leg PROPULSION during freestyle is often referred to as a SIX beat KICK.
5. Once the hand re-enters the water the hand should be placed in the CATCH position before starting the PULL.
6. Adding ROTATION to freestyle enhances technique, power, and efficiency.
7. The EXTENSION phase, maximizes the swimmers reach to help set up for an effective CATCH.

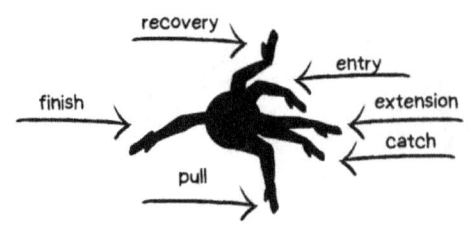

11. Lane Line Labyrinth pg19

12. Odd Ways To Train pg20

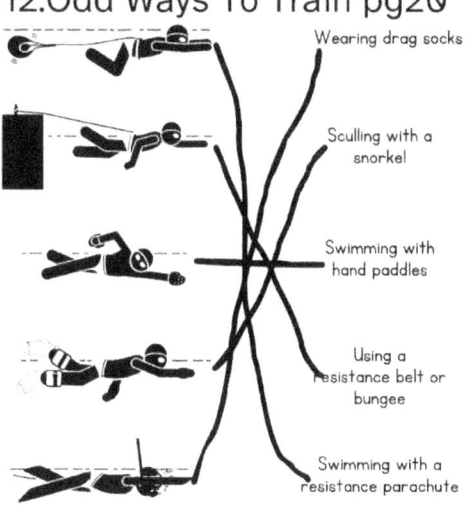

13. Lane Etiquette pg23

During training, always swim to the side of the contrasting LINE down the middle of the lane. It helps you swim straight and avoid collisions.

The underwater T at the end of the lane helps you know you are approaching the wall and when to TURN.

The FALSE START rope across the pool is there to help stop a race if someone goes too early.

When swimming backstroke count your strokes from the BACKSTROKE FLAGS to know where the wall is, this way, you won't BUMP your head.

The LANE ROPES are cables covered with small PLASTIC FLOATS, they have a contrasting color to indicate the RESURFACING POINT and to help swimmers see they are APPROACHING the end of the lane.

When you CIRCLE the lane, you swim in a clock-wise or counter-clockwise DIRECTION. This way, you won't bump into ONCOMING swimmers.

When training, never stop MID-LANE to fix goggles, roll onto your back, or wait until you reach the END of the lane.

To pass other swimmers, never grab their LEGS. Always pass on the OUTSIDE. People being passed should not SPEED UP, and should always move closer to the lane rope. This helps PREVENT COLLISIONS.

Always start your set with your feet touching the WALL, and always touch the wall with your HAND or hands when you finish a set. This gives you a chance to practice your race FINISHES.

When sharing a lane in training, as you finish a set, stop and MOVE TO THE SIDE so the next swimmer can FINISH AND TOUCH the wall.

When CONTINUING to swim, turn at the TARGET POINT - centered on the wall at the end of each lane then move immediately TO THE SIDE of the lane to AVOID COLLIDING with other swimmers.

Never DIVE IN unless the coach tells you to. Remember to ALWAYS look for swimmers before diving in, so you don't hurt OTHER SWIMMERS.

14. Swimming myth buster pg24

You should be able to see your knees break the surface when you kick on your back? **False**

Swimmers don't sweat? **False**

Swimming can turn your hair green? **True**

Swimming straight after eating a big lunch or milkshake will give you cramps? **True**

You should always sprint the warm-up? **False**

You should wait 15-30 minutes after applying sunscreen before going for a swim? **True**

The best swimmers hold their breath? **False**

It's OK to pee in the pool because everyone does it? **False**

Drills are a great way to pass the time and think about what's for dinner? **False**

Using a pull-buoy is a way for coach to let you rest your legs? **False**

Going too deep underwater can cause an ear infection? **True**

Swimming in a long-sleeve rashie can slow you down and make it hard to swim? **True**

There is only one way to swim freestyle? **False**

Swimming makes you sleepy and hungry? **True**

15. Find Their Fins Maze pg25

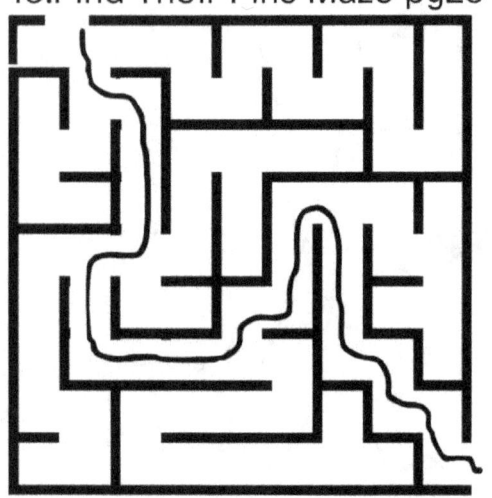

16. Pace Clock Facts & Phrases pg26

Leave On The Top: When the hand points to the "Top" or 60, swimmers begin their swim.
Leave On The Bottom: When the hand points to the "Bottom" or 30, swimmers begin their swim.
The time between swims or swimmers, often determined by the coach and the pace clock, is known as 'intervals'.
Second spacing is when the hand moves forward before the next swimmer starts their swim, ensuring consistent intervals.
The pace clock helps swimmers space out their leave times, maintaining control and consistency in rest intervals.
Swimmers get instant feedback on their swimming speed from the pace clock, helping them assess their performance
Using the pace clock helps swimmers see how they're improving and they can track their progress.

17. Breaststroke Brain Buster pg29

1. Answer Frog
2. Answer: Glide
3. Answer: Outsweep
4. Answer: Insweep
5. Answer: Recovery
6. Answer: Shoot

18. What's my time pg30

A: 35	D: 35s
B: 45	E: 15s
C: 10	

19. Race Finish and Turn Challenge pg31

How many hands do you touch the wall with for a freestyle finish?
a) One hand
Which strokes have a finish, where both hands must touch the wall simultaneously?
c) Butterfly & Breaststroke
What is the technique used for the butterfly-to-backstroke turn?
b) Open turn
In breaststroke, what is the rule for the finish?
a) Hands must be separated and touch the wall simultaneously
Which turn involves a transition from swimming on your back to swimming on your front?
a) Backstroke to breaststroke turn
Which two strokes commonly use flip turns to change direction at the wall?
d) Backstroke & Freestyle
A tumble turn is a different name for which of the two turns?
a) Flip turn and front flip

20. Get in the zone pg32

Recovery Zone 1 (Easy Swim)
Aerobic Zone 2 (Steady Swim)
Threshold Zone 3 (Challenge Yourself
VO2 Max Zone 4 (Push Your Limits)
Maximum effort Zone 5 (Give It Everything)

21. Locate Your Locker pg33

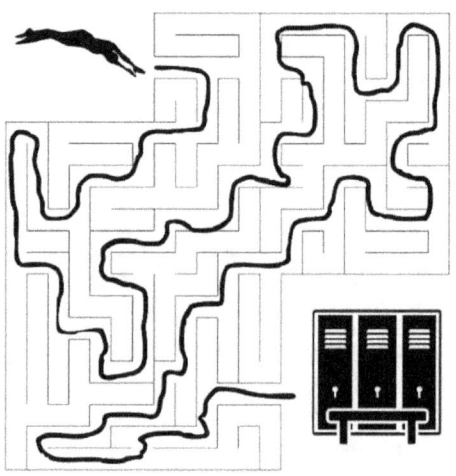

22. Butterfly True or False pg34

Butterfly kick is often referred to as dolphin kick? **TRUE**
There are only two kicks during the butterfly stroke cycle? **TRUE**
You should keep your eyes looking forward at all times when swimming butterfly? **FALSE**
It's ok if you swap the butterfly kick for the breaststroke kick when swimming butterfly if you get tired? **NEVER**
Swimming butterfly can help you swim better freestyle? **TRUE**
You should dive down as deep as you can when swimming butterfly? **FALSE**
The wave-like motion performed during butterfly is called the undulation? **TRUE**
The butterfly landing position is often referred to as the chest press? **TRUE**
Another name for swimming butterfly is the lady bird? **FALSE**
When swimming butterfly it is best to time the kicks with the hands as they enter and exit the water? **TRUE**
During the butterfly stroke, swimmers use a flutter kick? **FALSE**
When swimming butterfly, it's important to keep your head low and your body close to the water's surface? **TRUE**
Both hands exit the water near the hips when swimming butterfly? **TRUE**
Swimmers should pause and glide after the hands enter the water and before kicking during the butterfly stroke cycle? **FALSE**

23. Training aids pg35

T	J					L		P	
	E	A				O	S	A	
P		M	S			G		P	D
A		M	P	T	U	B		I	D	F
R		E	O	L		O		L	L
T		R	P	T		O		C	E	I
S		S	R	W		R	K	E	S	P
E		A	A			A		S		P
L	E		T				I	O		E
K			C					N		R
N			H						E	S
A	S	N	O	R	K	E	L			R

24. The I.M crossword puzzle pg36

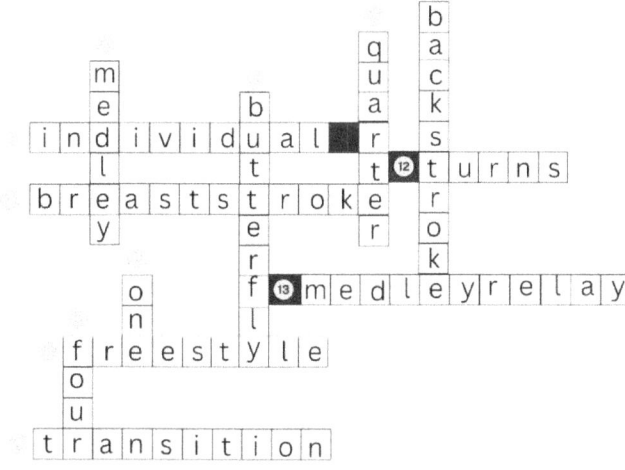

25. Jumbled Jargon pg37

vo2 max: The maximum amount of oxygen a person can use during intense exercise. It's like the engine capacity of a car!

negative split: Swimming the second half of a race faster than the first half. It's like pacing yourself to finish strong!

distance per stroke (DPS): How far you travel with each stroke. It's like measuring how efficient your swimming is!

personal best (PB): Your fastest time ever in a race. It's like beating your own record!

heat sheet: A list of swimmers and their events at a swim meet. It's like your race schedule!

intervals: Training sessions divided into timed segments of work and rest. It's like taking breaks between swimming hard!

lactate threshold: The point during exercise where lactic acid builds up in your muscles. It's like when your muscles start to feel tired!

critical swim speed (CSS): The pace at which you can swim continuously without getting tired too quickly. It's like finding your optimal swimming speed!

heartrate: The number of times your heart beats per minute. It's like a measure of how hard you're working!

stroke rate: The number of strokes you take per minute while swimming. It's like counting how fast you're arms are moving through the water

Thanks for diving into the 'Welcome To Squad' activity book!
We hope you had a splashing good time exploring the world of swimming training with us.

Stay in the swim of things by following us on Instagram @learntoswimtheaustralianway for more swimming tips, updates, and fun content.

And if you're hungry for more aquatic adventures, don't forget to check out our other books from the Learn To Swim The Australian Way Series on our website www.borntoswim.com.au
There's a sea of knowledge waiting for you!

Plus, gear up for your next swim session with our exclusive merchandise for swimmers at www.poweredbychlorine.com
From swim gear to stylish apparel, we've got everything you need to make a splash in and out of the pool.

www.ingramcontent.com/pod-product-compliance
Lightning Source LLC
Chambersburg PA
CBHW082214070526
44585CB00020B/2414